The BIG Book of Berenstain Bears BEGINNER BOOKS

Stan & Jan Berenstain

Random House 🏠 New York

Contents

The Bears' Picnic   5

The Bear Detectives   68

The Berenstain Bears and

    the Missing Dinosaur Bone   108

The Big Honey Hunt   149

The Bear Scouts   213

The Bike Lesson   277

The Bears' PICNIC

by **Stan and Jan Berenstain**

Mother Bear,
put your apron away.
We are going to go
on a picnic today!

Where are we going
on our picnic, Dad?

To the very best place
in the world, my lad!

Now you remember
this spot, my dear.
When we were young,
we picnicked here.

Papa, I do not
like to complain,
but your wonderful spot
is next to a train!

Where are we going
now, Papa Bear?
Is there another
wonderful spot somewhere?

Don't pester me
with questions, please.
There's a place I know
right in those trees.

It is everything
a picnic spot should be.
And no one remembers
it is here but me.

What a spot! What a spot!
So quiet! So cool!
Just as it was
when I was in school.

We had a school picnic
and I won first place
for eating the most pie
in a pie-eating race.

Pop, this spot may
be very fine,
but look what it says
on that big sign!

Dad,
can you find us
another spot?
Are we having
a picnic
today, or not?

22

Now stop asking questions!
Be quiet! Stop stewing!
Your father knows
what he is doing.

To pick a spot that is
just the right one,
you have to be very
choosy, my son.

Nothing can bother
our picnic here!
Lay out the picnic
things, my dear.

I do not like
to say so, Dad,
but another good spot
has just gone bad.

I hope there's another
good spot you know.
But how much farther
do we have to go?

Why don't you use
your eyes, Small Bear?
There's a perfect place
right over there!

The grass is green.
The air is sweet.
Lay out the lunch,
and take a seat.

Hooray!
At last
we're going to eat!

Well . . .

this place is good.

I wasn't wrong.

But I know one better.

Let's move along.

37

Now take this perfect
piece of ground.
No one but us
for miles around!

Pop, you picked
the best spot yet.
But how can we picnic
with that jet?

I am very
hungry, Pop!
When is this spot-picking
going to stop?

I am getting tired.
My feet hurt, too.
Any old spot here
ought to do.

Please, Pop, please,
can't we picnic soon?
It's long past lunch.
It's afternoon!

You have to be choosy,
Pop, I know.
But what's better up here
than down below?

What's up here? . . .
I'll tell you what.
The world's most perfect
picnic spot!

As you can see,
it is perfectly clear
that *nothing* can bother
our picnic here.

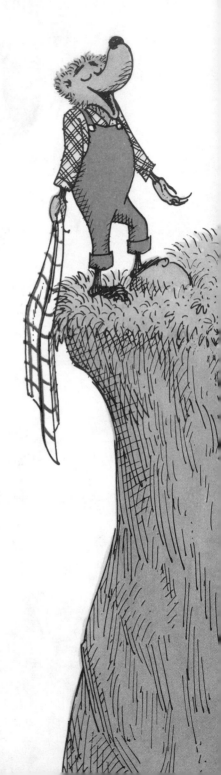

No noisy crowds!
No pesky planes!
And no mosquitoes,
trucks or trains!

Oh-oh, Dad.

Here come the rains!

Pooh!
Rain to a bear
is nothing at all.
We'll picnic here
and let it fall.

Come back!

What kind of bears are you?

Scared of a drop

of rain or two!

Bring back that food!

This place will do.

It's dry in here.

It's warm here, too!

It does look warm.

Yes, I agree.

But it looks much, much
too warm for me!

Wait, now! Wait!
You wait for me!
I'll find a better spot.
You'll see.

I'll find the perfect
place to eat.
I'll find a spot
that can't be beat!
The finest spot
you've ever seen....

Now,
THAT
is the kind
of place I mean!

He did it,
Mother.
Did he not?
He found the perfect
picnic spot!

DETECTIVES

THE CASE OF THE MISSING PUMPKIN

Jan Berenstain

Help!
My pumpkin won
first prize at the fair.
Now I can't find it
anywhere!

Do not worry,
Farmer Ben.
The BEAR DETECTIVES
will find it again!

THE
BEAR
DETECTIVES

Your prize pumpkin stolen?
Never fear.
Great Bear Detective Pop is here!
I will find it.
You will see.

Just watch
my old dog Snuff and me.

But, Papa,
our Bear Detective Book
will tell us how
to catch the crook.

"Lesson One.
First look around
for any TRACKS
that are on the ground."

Don't waste your time
with books and stuff!
We're on the trail!
Just follow Snuff!

We'll catch that crook.
We'll show you how.
Snuff and I
will catch the . . .

. . . cow?

Say! Look down there!
Do you see what I see?

There's a
WHEELBARROW TRACK
going by this tree!

A good detective
writes things down:

"Checked out a cow,
white and brown."

The track ends here.
What shall we do?

We'll look in the book.

It says,
"Lesson Two.
Look all around
for another clue.'

Humf! You can look around
as much as you please.
I'm going to follow
these carrots and peas . . .

. . . and eggshells
and corncobs
and other stuff.

This must be the way!
Let's go, Snuff!

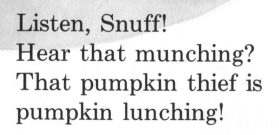

MUNCH MUNCH CRUNCH GOBBLE

Listen, Snuff!
Hear that munching?
That pumpkin thief is
pumpkin lunching!

O.K., thief!
You've munched your last.
Your pumpkin-stealing
days are past.

Look here! Look here,
Papa Bear.
We found a new clue
over there.

You see
we found
a PUMPKIN LEAF . . .

Aha!
You've found a pumpkin leaf.
Just show me where
you found this leaf.
Then I will find that
pumpkin thief.

The pumpkin thief!
I've found him, Snuff!
Let's grab him quick.
He sure looks tough.

Be careful, Pop.
Lesson Three in the book
says, "Before you leap,
be sure to look."

Hang on, Snuff!
Hold him tight!
This pumpkin thief
can really fight.

Did you find any clues
in that scarecrow, Pop?
Shall we keep on looking,
or shall we stop?

Hmmmmmmmmm . . .
Checked out a cow,
three pigs in a pen,
and a scarecrow owned
by Farmer Ben.

Found some tracks
and a pumpkin leaf.
Still haven't found
that pumpkin thief.

Look! By that haystack!
I see something blue!
It's the first-prize ribbon.
That's a very good clue!

A haystack!
The perfect place
to hide.

I'll bet the thief
is right inside.

Pumpkin thief,
don't try to run.
Your pumpkin-stealing
days are done!

But, Papa . . .

I was trying to say,
I don't think the thief
is in THAT hay.

Hmmmmmm . . .
Ben's haystack
is another spot
where the pumpkin thief
is not.

Say! Look over there!
Look in that door!
PUMPKIN SEEDS
all over the floor!

He's in the barn! This is it!
Hand me that detective kit.

I'll snap on these handcuffs.
I'll take him to jail.
Pumpkin thief,
it's the end of the trail.

Old Snuff,
this may be tough.

It looks
like we've caught
a whole GANG
of crooks.

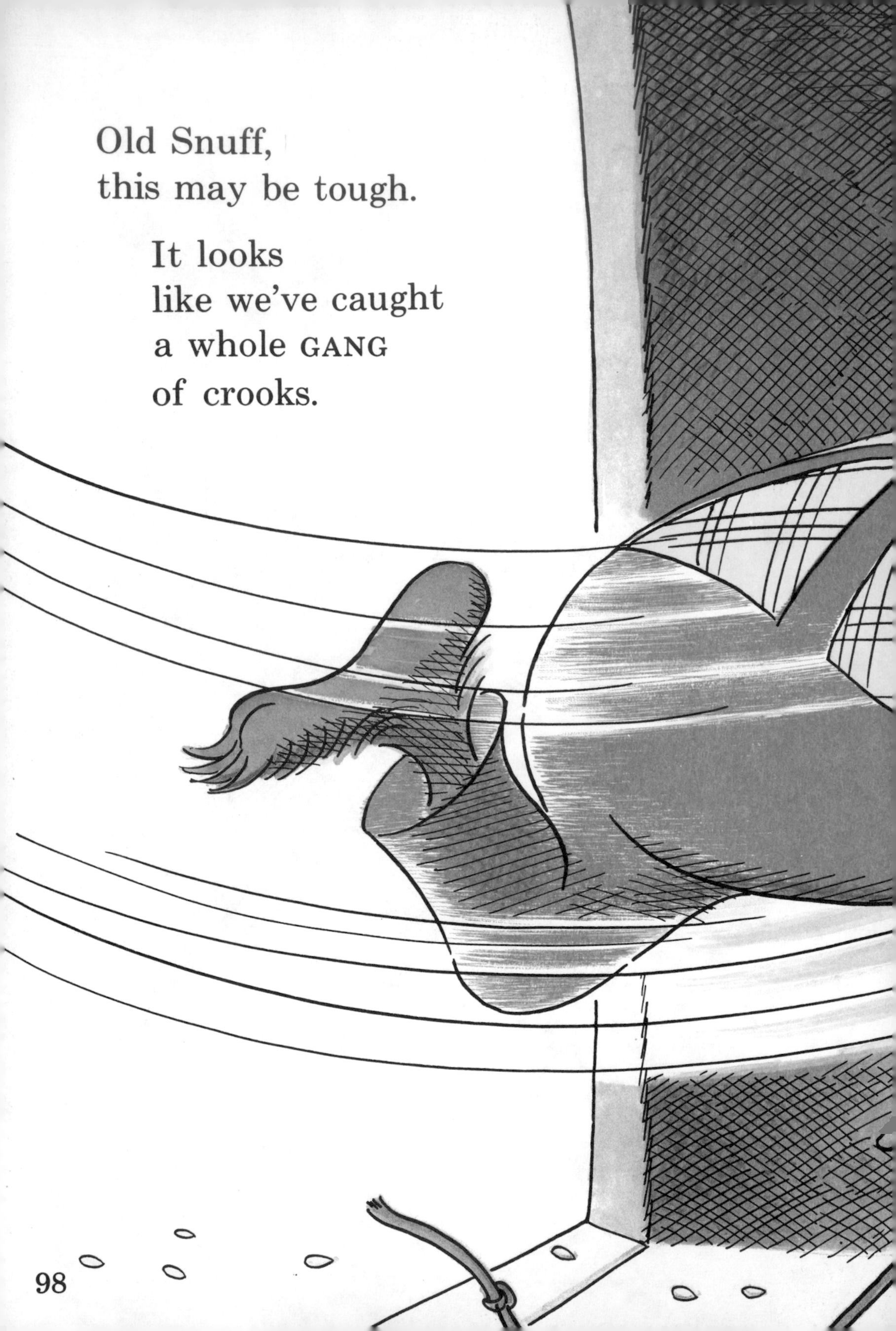

Hmmmmm . . .
Checked out a cow,
brown and white.
Checked out a scarecrow
after a fight.

Checked out a haystack.
Three pigs in a pen . . .
Put the cuffs on
Farmer Ben's hen.

Found some tracks,
a ribbon, a leaf . . .
some pumpkin seeds,

BUT STILL
NO THIEF!

Small Bear, I guess you better look
at what it says there in your book.

Lesson Four—
here's how it goes—
"A good detective
will USE HIS NOSE!"

Hmmmmmmm . . .
Pumpkin seeds,
pumpkin shell—
and . . .
aha!
I smell a
PUMPKIN SMELL!

The pumpkin was pied
by Mrs. Ben.

The case is solved.
Good work, men!
The BEAR DETECTIVES
have done it again!

MMMMMMM!
My dear, you and I
will SHARE first prize.
ME for the pumpkin,
YOU for the pies!

The Berenstain Bears and the Missing DINOSAUR

Stan and Jan Berenstain

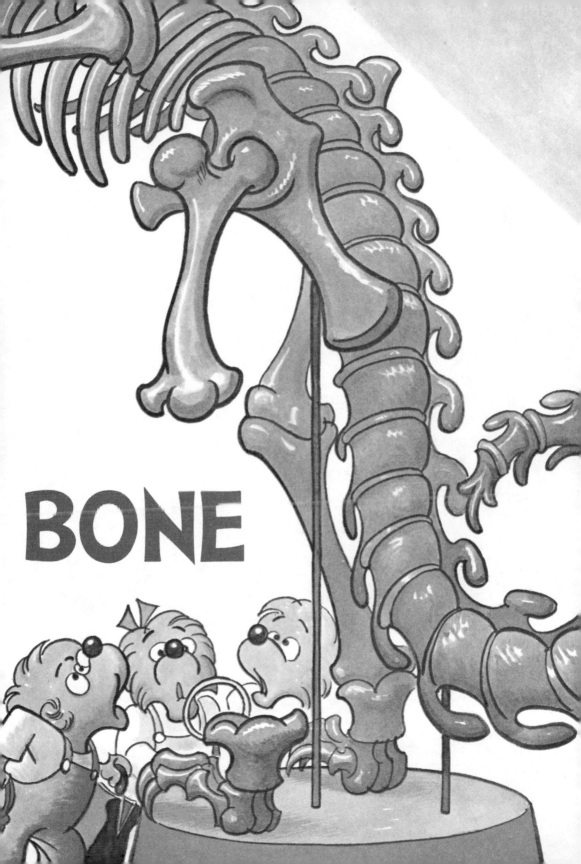

Bears lining up
outside the door.

Dr. Bear, inside,
pacing the floor.

What's wrong in there?

What's up? What's up?

wonder three little bears

and one little pup.

A dinosaur bone
is missing in there!
"Somebody took it!"
said Dr. Bear.
"Who took that bone?
Who took it? Where?"

Three little bears
and their hound dog, Snuff,
come inside
with their detective stuff.

There's no case too hard,
no case too tough,
for the Bear Detectives
and their hound dog, Snuff!

The search begins!
And none too soon.
The Bear Museum
opens at noon.

They will search the place.

Every cranny and nook.

Will they find the bone?

Will they find the crook?

A dark, dark room.

A mummy's tomb!

Is that the thief?

That spooky face?

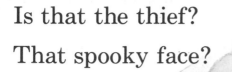

The MUMMY ROOM

No.

That's the museum's

mummy case.

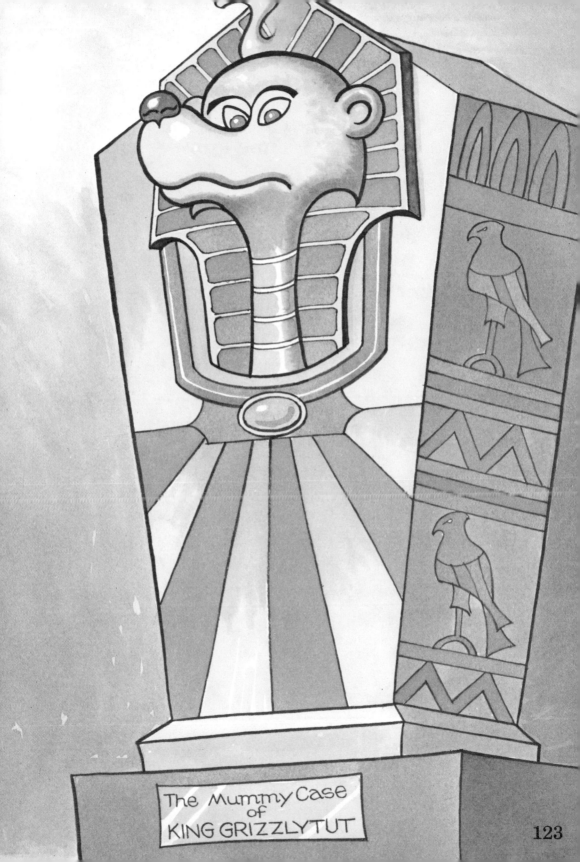

Eleven fifteen.

Time grows short.

OPEN
AT
NOON

Now, where would one hide
a bone of that sort?

It could be there,
inside that vase.
The bone thief's
perfect hiding place!

VALUABLE
VASE

"You can look
in that valuable vase
if you must.
There's nothing
in there
but some valuable dust."

Not much time left.
Just half an hour!
The Bear Detectives
search the tower.

There he is! The thief!

And the bone he stole!

Wrong again.

That's an

Indian totem pole.

It's getting late
but still they look.
And still no bone,
and still no crook.

"Say . . .

maybe bone thieves work in packs.

Three thieves!

With a sword, and a gun, and an ax!"

Wrong again!

It's the museum's

famous statues of wax!

GENGHIS
BEAR

QUEEN
FLIZABEAR

They had better find
that leg bone soon.
There's just one minute
left till noon!

With no more time
to search and look,
they know they will not
catch that crook.

They failed!
This case is much too hard. . . .

Wait! . . .

What's that out there

in the yard?

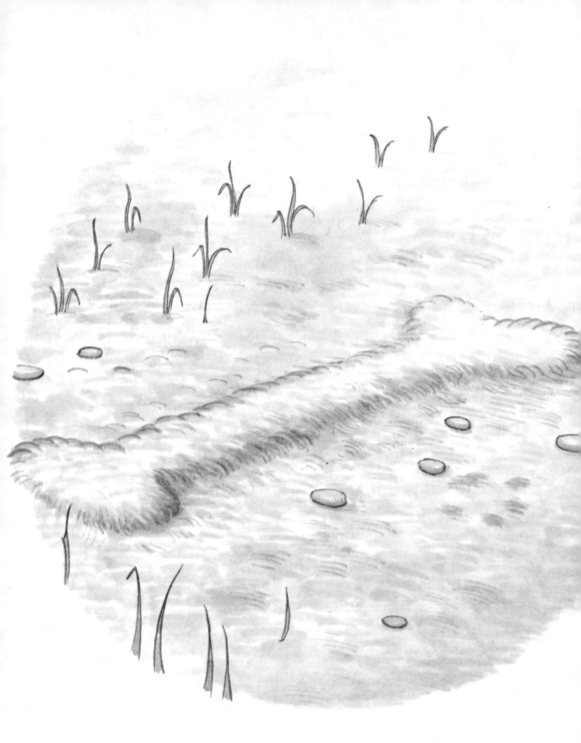

That lump of ground—
that bone-shaped mound!

The missing bone!
It's found! It's found!

With hound dog paw prints
all around.

THE CASE IS SOLVED!

No job's too hard,
no case too tough,
for the Bear Detectives . . .

and that

bone thief, Snuff.

The
Big
Honey
Hunt

by Stanley and Janice Berenstain

We ate our honey.

We ate a lot.

Now we have no honey

In our honey pot.

Go get some honey.

Go get some more.

Go get some honey

From the honey store.

We will go for honey.
Come on, Small Bear!
We will go for honey
And I know where.

The store . . .
She said to
Get it there!

Not at the store.

Oh, no, Small Bear.

If a bear is smart,

If a bear knows how,

He goes on a honey hunt.

Watch me now!

How do you hunt it?

How, Dad, how?

If a bear knows how,
If a bear is smart,
He looks for a bee
Right at the start.

Bees hide their honey
In trees that are hollow.
So we will find
A bee to follow.

Is that a bee?

He went, "Buzz! Buzz!"

B-Z-Z-Z

He looks like a bee.

Why, yes!

He does.

B-Z-Z-Z

We will follow that bee . . .

We will follow that bee . . .

B-Z-Z-Z

We will follow that bee
To his honey tree.

That tree!

Is that a honey tree?

B-Z-Z-Z

It looks like one
So I know it's one.
Sit down, Small Bear,
And watch the fun.
Small Bear, you watch
Your smart old Dad
Take out more honey
Than you ever had.

B-Z-Z-Z

Are you getting honey?
Are you getting a lot?
Will we take home honey
In our honey pot?

B-Z-Z-Z

That is not
A honey bee!
That was not
A honey tree.

B-Z-Z-Z

B-Z-Z-Z

The bee!

The bee!

There goes the bee!

On with the honey hunt!
Follow your Pop.
Your Pop will find honey
At the very next stop.

B-Z-Z-Z

We will follow, and follow . . .

And follow along!

I will find a new tree
And I won't be wrong.

Is that a honey tree?

How do you know?

Well, it looks just so.

And it feels just so.

Looks so. Feels so.

So it's SO!

Now watch, Small Bear.

I am about

To take that

Good old honey out.

173

How are you doing?

Are you getting a lot?

Are you getting much honey?

Or are you not?

BZ-Z-Z

Wrong kind of tree!
Wrong kind of tree!

Look, Dad!
There goes
Your friend the bee!

B-Z-Z-Z

On with the hunt!
I will not rest.
I will follow that bee
To his honey nest!

When a bear is smart,
When a bear is clever,
He never gives up.
And I won't, ever!

B-Z-Z-Z

Dad!
Is that
A bee tree there?

181

I know it is.

Why, yes, Small Bear.

It can't be wrong

Like the last tree was.

Only a bee tree

Goes, "Buzz! Buzz!"

Are you getting honey?
Are you doing well?
Or is something wrong?
I smell a smell.

B-Z-Z

The bee!
The bee!
I see the bee!

If you want to get honey,
There is just one way.
You must follow your bee
If it takes all day.

If a bear is smart,
If a bear is bright,
A bear keeps going
If it takes all night.

He went in there!
Your friend the bee!
He went in there!
Is this our tree?

Now let me think.

Now let me see . . .

This looks just like

A honey tree.

And . . .
    It feels
    Just like
    A honey tree.

And . . .

It goes, "Buzz! Buzz!"

Like a honey tree.

B-Z-Z

195

B-Z-Z-Z

B-Z-Z-Z

-Z

-Z-Z-Z

And . . .

It tastes

Just like

A honey tree!

And so

You see

This tree must be—

Must, must, must be

A honey tree!

I never saw
More honey! Never!
Now don't you think
Your Dad is clever?

I think you are
Very clever, Dad.
But your friends the bees
Are very mad!

But Dad!
You left
The honey there!

It was not
The kind I want,
Small Bear.

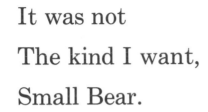

I will get you honey.

I said I would.

But that bee's honey

Was not too good.

Where are you going
To find the honey?
Here in the water?
Now that seems funny.

No, we won't find honey
In here, Small Bear.
But soon, very soon
I will show you where.
When the bees have gone,
We will get along, too.
Your Dad is smart,
And he knows what to do.

But how will you
Do it, Dad?
How, Dad? How?

The best sort of honey
Never comes from bees.
It comes from a store.
I would like some,
Please.

The Bear Scouts

by Stan and Jan Berenstain

Good-bye, Bear Scouts!
Good luck! Have fun!
Isn't Dad going camping
With you, Son?

Not this time.
We don't need Pa.
We've got the Bear Scout
Guidebook, Ma.
It tells us all
We need to know
About camping out
And where to go.

A guidebook, Son?

Now, wait a minute!

I know more

Than the book has in it.

A smart bear opens
His eyes wide
And never needs
A Bear Scout Guide.

Now, Son, stop.
Right here you'll see
Just why you need
A guide like me!

What would you do,
My fine young scout,
To get across
When a bridge is out?

The book says first,

"In such a spot . . .

Tie your rope

With a Bear Scout knot."

Scout knot—bah!

A smart bear knows

He has no need

For one of those.

He ties his *own* knot

To the tree

And safely crosses.

Now watch me.

221

We're here, Scouts.
But Dad is not!
What has happened
To his knot?

224

On second thought—
I'll stay with you.
So I can show you
What to do.
That camp ground is so far,
You see,
You really need
A guide like me.

Look here, Bear Scouts.
Your book can't show
Which way is
The way to go.
But a bear like me,
A bear who's clever,
Takes the short way.
The long way? Never!

But, Papa, wait!
Here's a map in the book.
It says to go
The long way. Look!

Well, you'll find me
At the other end.
A smart bear takes
The short way, friend.

On second thought,
I'll come along.
Just in case
Something goes wrong.

Now that I've brought you
Safely here,
We'll get down this river.
Never fear.

Yes, Papa. Look.
Here's a plan in the book.

It shows us all
We need to do . . .

To build a fine
Bear Scout canoe.

Build a canoe?
That takes too long!
A bear who's smart
Will know that's wrong.
It's easy to see
That's much too slow.
I know a faster
Way to go.

So long, Bear Scouts!
Toodle-oo!
You can have
Your slow canoe.

I never like
To wait around.
I'll meet you
At the camping ground.

We're coming, Dad!
Just grab the rope.
The Guidebook says
There's always hope.

On second thought—
I'll go with you.
Then I can show you
What to do.
If you go on
And I do not,
You'll never find
Your camping spot.

You won't need
The Guidebook now.
Here's where I really
Show you how.
For this is where
We set up camp,
And I'm the world's
Camp set-up champ!

Now watch this.
I'm really good
At starting a fire
By rubbing wood.

Excuse me, Dad.

That way's not right.

The book says

That will take all night.

We'll try this way.
It ought to light.
Look! Now our fire
Is burning bright.

Bear Scouts, you're
Going to have a treat.
I'll cook you something
Good to eat.

A wise bear knows
There's a meal to be found
Wherever he is,
If he just looks around.

I'll put in some eggs
And fresh green weeds.
Some toadstools. Then
Some roots and leaves.
And presto, chango,
Ala kazoo . . .
That's how I make
My favorite stew.

Dad, your stew
Is stewing well.
But doesn't it have
A funny smell?

Besides, the book says,
"For the best camp dish,
Take your rods
And catch some fish."

On second thought—
I'll share your meal.
My stew's a bit
Too rich, I feel.

Now, Scouts, you'll find
A bear who's bright
Will make his bed
While it's still light.

The Guidebook says—
Page eighty-eight—
"Put up your tents
Before it's late."

Tents are for sissies!
Be smart, be brave!
You haven't camped out
Till you've slept
in a cave.

Ow! That was quite
A fall I took.
You'd better come
And

BRING

THAT

BOOK!

We're coming, Dad.
No need to worry.
We'll have you mended
In a hurry.

First, bandage nose,
Then thumb, then head.
Then put me
On a rescue sled.

Well done, Bear Scouts!
We're nearly there,
Thanks to your
Smart old Papa Bear.
As I have told you
All along,
With a guide like me,
You can't go wrong.

Dad has shown us
Quite a lot
About what's smart
And what is not.

The Bike Lesson

by
Stan and Jan Berenstain

Come here, Small Bear.
Here is something
you will like.

Look, Ma, look!
A brand-new bike.

Thanks, Dad! Thanks!
For me, you say?
I am going to ride it
right away!

Not yet, not yet,
not yet, my son . . .

First come the lessons,
then the fun.
How to get on is
lesson one.

Lesson one?

Is that lesson one?

Yes.
That is what
you should not do.
So let that be a
lesson to you.

Dad! Where are you going?

You showed me how.

Why don't you let me

ride it now?

Yes it was, Dad.
Now I see.
That was a very good
lesson for me.

Not yet. Not yet.
Before you do
I'll have to give you
lesson two.

Just watch, Small Bear.
Just watch your Pop.
Lesson two is
how to stop.

A very good lesson.
Thank you, Pop.

May I ride it now
that you showed me how?
May I?
May I ride it now?

Not yet. Not yet.

You have more to learn.

I'll have to show you

how to turn.

Just watch me . . .

This is lesson
number three.

Wow! What a lesson!

That number three!

That may be a little

too hard for me.

This is what
you must never do.
Now let this be
a lesson to you.

It surely was, Dad!

Now I see.

That was a very good

lesson for me.

When I get you down
may I ride it then?
May I? May I?
Just say when.

Wait, my son.

You must learn some more.

I have yet to teach

you lesson four.

When you come to a puddle
what will you do?
Will you go around
or ride right through?

It's not so good
to ride right through.

You're right, Dad.
I can clearly see
why that lesson
was good for me.

When I get you out,
may I ride it then?
Please, Dad . . .
Will you tell me when?

Of course. You may ride it.
You can. You will.

. . . After lesson five.

How to go down hill.

Wow! What a lesson!
That looks hard,
going down hill
through a chicken yard.

313

Dad, please tell me . . . will I
ever get to ride it?
Or will I just keep
running beside it?

Pretty soon, Son.

But not just yet.

There is still one lesson

you have to get.

Lesson six is

the hardest yet.

To be a good rider,
to really know how,
you will have to learn
about safety now.

To be safe, Small Bear,
when you ride a bike,
you can not just take
any road you like.

Before you take one
you must know . . .

. . . where that road
is going to go.

See?
This is what
you should not do.
Now let this be
a lesson to you.

It surely was, Dad.

Now I see.

That was another good

lesson for me.

May I ride it now?
May I ride it now?

After one more lesson.

It will be the last.

There is one more thing.

I can teach it fast.

When I ride on a road
I take great pride
in always riding
on the right hand side.

But, Dad!
Are you riding
on the right hand side?

I guess I know
my hands, Small Bear.
My right is here.
My left is there.

Or am I wrong?

Now could that be?

Left hand . . . ? Right hand . . . ?

Let me see . . .

Left hand on the
left hand side . . .
Right hand on the
right hand side.

Thank you, Pop!

You showed me how.

But, please

please

PLEASE

may I ride it now?

Look, Ma!
Now I can ride it!
See!
Dad had some very good
lessons for me.